Simon James

Nurse Clementine

It was Clementine Brown's birthday.
Mr and Mrs Brown bought her
a nurse's outfit and a first aid kit.

"It's just what I wanted," she said.

"You can call me 'Nurse Clementine' from now on!"

Nurse Clementine didn't have to wait long for her first emergency.

Mr Brown banged his toe on the living room door.

Straight away Nurse Clementine got to work.
"You'll need to keep this on for a week," she said.
"A week?" moaned Mr Brown.
"A week," said Nurse Clementine firmly.

Next, Mrs Brown
complained she had
a headache.
Nurse Clementine
gave her a complete
check-up.

Her ears were okay,
her tongue wasn't
spotty and her
temperature
was normal.

So, just to be safe, Nurse Clementine bandaged her head.

"You'll have to keep this on for a week," she said.

"A week?" sighed Mrs Brown.

"A week," said Nurse Clementine firmly.

In the kitchen,
Nurse Clementine
found Wellington
licking his paw.

It must be sore, decided
Nurse Clementine.
She bandaged it up
as best she could.

Nurse Clementine was very pleased with her work. She rushed off to find her brother Tommy. He was bound to need some help.

Bold and fearless, Tommy the superhero
was on his way down the stairs.

"Look out, Tommy!" shouted Clementine.
"You're going to hit—

the door!" Nurse Clementine immediately opened her first aid kit. "It's a good job I'm here," she said.

"No, it's not!" said Tommy. "I don't need a nurse."

"I'm Super Tommy, watch me fly.
I can leap from sofas."

"Oh, look out, Tommy!"
said Clementine.
"You're going to hit—

the floor!"
"Ouch!" said Tommy.

Nurse Clementine rushed over with her stethoscope. She told Tommy to keep still while she checked him for breaks and bruises.

"I'm not broken," said Tommy. "And I told you before, I *don't* need a nurse. Leave me alone!"

Tommy marched off towards the garden.

Clementine sat while Tommy played.

There was no one left to take care of.

She would just have to practise nursing by herself.
First, she listened for her own heartbeat.

Then, she practised bandaging on the drainpipe.

But it was no good.
"Nurses need someone to look after," Clementine sighed.

Then, she heard a voice calling
from up in the tree.
"Clementine! Clementine!
It's me," said Tommy.

“I’m stuck!” he cried. “I can’t get down –
it’s too high!”

“Hang on, Tommy!”
called Clementine,
“I’ll get you down.”

Clementine knew
she had to think
quickly.

After all, this was
a **real** emergency.

Clementine was on tiptoe but she couldn't reach Tommy.

"I'm slipping," he said.

"Hold on," said Nurse Clementine.

"I can't!" said Tommy. "I'm going to fall."

Tommy closed his eyes as his hands slipped.
But Nurse Clementine was there to catch him.
"I've got you," she said.

Tommy was relieved to be back on the ground.
"Thanks, Clementine," he said, "you were great!"

When Tommy turned
to go, Clementine
noticed something.
"Tommy," she said.
"You've grazed
your arm!"
"Have I?" said Tommy.

"You can bandage
it if you like."

Nurse Clementine
was delighted to help.
This was going to be
her best bandage yet.
But there was one
small problem ...

she had forgotten her scissors!

“This is going to be an extra special superhero bandage,” said Nurse Clementine.

“Really?” said Tommy.

“But you’re going to have to keep it on *all* week,” said Clementine, firmly.

"All week?" said Tommy. "Great!"

The End

Simon James

ISBN 978-1-4063-3842-3

Simon James is an award-winning author and illustrator of books for children – creator of the much-loved character Baby Brains and of touching tales exploring a child's unique relationship with nature.

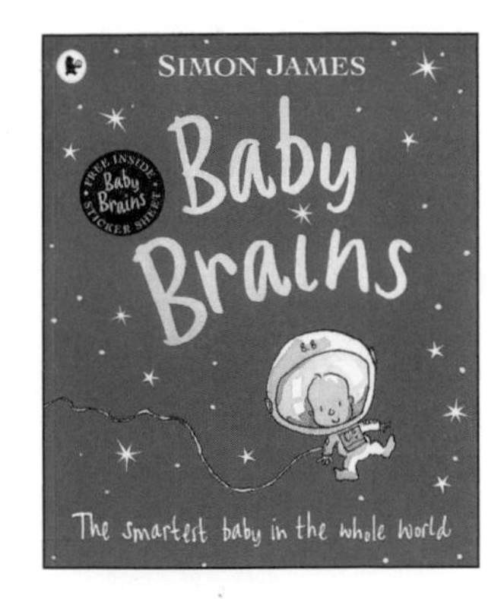

ISBN 978-1-84428-522-8

ISBN 978–1-4063-4103-4

ISBN 978-1-4063-0846-4

ISBN 978-1-4063-0848-8

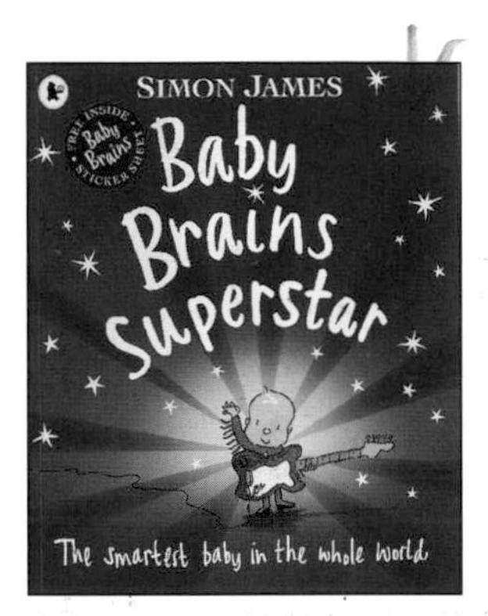

ISBN 978-1-4063-0202-8

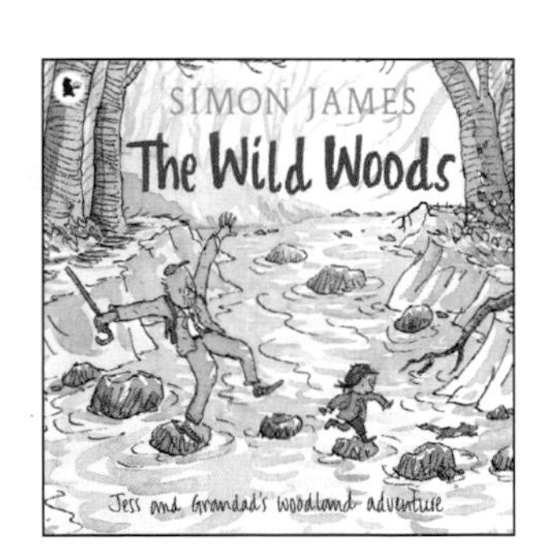

ISBN 978–1-4063-0845-7

ISBN 978-1-4063-0849-5

ISBN 978-1-84428-467-2

ISBN 978-1-4063-1338-3

"Drawing always opens up a very private and delightful world. It's easy to forget that drawing in itself is a kind of magic. Drawing is good for you!" Simon James